MISSION 1

OXYGEN LEVEL ZERO

MARS DIARIES

MISSION 1

OXYGEN LEVEL ZERO

SIGMUND BROUWER

TYNDALE KIDS

TYNDALE HOUSE PUBLISHERS, INC.
WHEATON, ILLINOIS

Visit Tyndale's exciting Web site for kids at www.marsdiaries.com

Designed by Justin Ahrens

Edited by Ramona Cramer Tucker

ISBN 0-8423-4304-0

Printed in the United States of America

06   05   04   03   02   01
9   8   7   6   5   4   3

CHAPTER 1

Sandstorm!

Across the plains, the black shell of the gigantic dome gleamed in late-afternoon sunshine. It was beautiful against the red soil, laden with iron oxides, and the faded rose-colored Martian sky. From the bottom of the mountain where I stood, it took less than an hour's trek across the plains to reach it—in good weather.

But we would not get that hour. Sand rattled hard against my titanium casing, warning me of how little time remained. Much less than we needed.

I turned my head to the left, into the wind that raked the sand across me. A huge dark wall lifted from the north of the plains, a blanket of doom that covered more and more of the sky. Winds of near-hurricane force lifted tons upon tons of red sand particles. Already the front edge of the storm reached out to us. In less than half an hour, those tons of sand would begin to cover me and the three scientists I had been sent out of the dome to find.

"Home base," I called into my radio. "This is Rescue Force One. Please make contact. Home base. This is Rescue Force One. Please make contact."

There was no answer. Just like there had been no answer the other hundred times I'd tried in the last half-hour.

A solar flare must have knocked out the satellite beam. The sun was 140 million miles away, so weak and so far from Mars that on winter nights, the temperature here dropped down to minus two hundred degrees Fahrenheit. Yet all it took was a storm on the surface of the sun to fire out electromagnetic streams nearing the speed of light, and communication systems all through the entire solar system would pay the price.

"Home base," I said. "This is Rescue Force One. Please make contact."

One of the scientists walked in front of me, blocking my view of the base. He leaned down and pushed his helmet visor into my forward video lens.

"What are we going to do?" he shouted.

He did not have to shout. I could hear him clearly.

Nor did he have to walk around in front of me. I could have seen him just as easily with my rear video lens. Or one of my side lenses.

"Forward," I said. "We cannot stop."

"No! We must make shelter."

Did he think I had not thought of this already?

Standard procedure in dealing with a sandstorm was to go to high ground, unfold an emergency pop-up blanket, and crawl beneath it. The pop-up blanket made a miniature dome that would easily provide shelter for as many days as it took the storm to pass. But fools who used the pop-up blanket on low ground would be buried by the sand, never to be found again.

"Forward," I said. "Follow me."

"That's easy for you!" he shouted. "You're just a stupid machine!"

He was correct both times. It would be easy for me to travel in a sandstorm. And I was just a machine.

But he was also wrong. I was more than a machine. And I was not stupid. I knew plenty.

I knew that during each Martian fall and winter, the carbon dioxide gas in the atmosphere froze out of the air and onto the ground, making a giant hood of frost that covered from the pole to the equator. I knew that as spring arrived, the difference in temperatures between the sun-warmed soil and the retreating ice made for fierce winds. I knew these strong winds were so monstrous that sometimes sandstorms covered the entire planet. I knew if we took shelter, we might be trapped for days.

I also knew that the last scientist of the three only had ten hours of oxygen left in his tank. If we took shelter, he would die long before the storm ended.

"One of you will die if we stop," I said. "If we continue, all of you will survive."

"We'll get lost in the storm! No one survives a sandstorm."

"No," I insisted. "My navigation system is intact. We will link ourselves by cable, and I will maintain direction. All you need to do is follow."

"No!" he yelled. "Not through a sandstorm!"

"Listen," I said, "if we stop, he has no chance."

"Should three of us die instead of one?" The scientist picked up a rock and tried to smash it against my head. But since he wore a big atmosphere suit and was very slow, I moved out of the way easily.

He picked up another rock and threw it at me. I put up my arms to protect my video lenses, and the rock clanged off my elbows. The other two scientists watched, doing nothing. They were very tired. I had rescued them from the bottom of a giant sinkhole where they had been stranded for two days.

The first scientist picked up another rock to throw. It was a big rock. Even though his suit made him clumsy, he would be able to throw it hard. Mars has very little gravity compared to Earth. A person throwing a rock the size of a grapefruit on Earth could easily throw a rock the size of a basketball on Mars.

What was I going to do?

If I let the scientist with the rocks force us to stop and put up a shelter, one of them would die.

But if I grabbed the scientist with the rock in my sharp metal claws, I would most certainly poke a hole in his space suit. With an atmosphere of 95 percent carbon dioxide, he would die within minutes.

Either way, it didn't look like I could find a way to make sure all three scientists made it back to the dome alive. I would fail in my task. I could not allow that.

Another rock clanged off my leg.

"No!" I said. "No!"

This was getting worse. If I ran off to protect myself, then all three of them might die. But if I stayed to try to protect them, one of those rocks might smash and disable me. Which would mean all three of them might die.

I couldn't decide what to do.

The scientist threw another rock. It hit my shoulder.

A huge blast of sand swept over us. For a brief moment, I could see nothing in any direction from my four video lenses.

In the instant the air cleared again, I saw the scientist with another rock in his fist. But it was too late. Out of the swirling sand he appeared, aiming the rock toward my video lenses.

. The rock smashed down.

The rose-colored Martian sky tilted. The red soil zoomed toward me. Then everything went black. . . .

CHAPTER 2

"Ouch," I said.

I opened my eyes to the square, sterile room of the computer simulation lab. I was under the dome, not outside of it, stuck in a raging sandstorm.

That was the good news.

The bad news was that although no rock had actually hit my body, my head did hurt. That's the way it is with a virtual-reality program. It's like a computer game. Except you're actually in the game. Instead of watching your players get knocked out, it happens in a small way to you.

I pulled the surround-sight helmet off my head. My hair was slick with sweat. The concentration it took to move the virtual-reality robot controls by flexing my own muscles was hard work. It didn't help that I was also wearing a one-piece jacket and gloves, wired with thousands of tiny cables that reacted to every movement I made. I'd been in the computer program for five hours, and that jacket held every scrap of my body heat.

"*Ouch* is right," Rawling McTigre said, looking up from his own screen where he sat at a desk across the cramped room from me. "My readout shows he cracked three video lenses and shocked your computer drive. Basically, he killed you. A human defeating a robot."

Rawling McTigre, one of the two medical doctors under the dome, was stocky and had wide shoulders and short dark hair streaked with gray. He said his hair had turned gray from trying to look after me. I spent so much time with him, there were days when I wished he were my father. I mean, because voice-to-voice calls were far too costly as my real father traveled between Earth and Mars, and because the round trip took so long, all I really had for a father was a photo of some guy in a pilot's space suit.

"What were you thinking out there?" Rawling asked.

"Thinking? I didn't have time to think," I responded. "I'd spent four hours tracking them down and suddenly the one idiot decides he doesn't want to be rescued. Besides, who programmed the sandstorm into this rescue operation? Wasn't it bad enough one guy is running low on oxygen and the satellite communications are down? What was next—a short circuit that left my robot unit with only one arm or one video lens in operation?"

"Tyce, Tyce, Tyce." Rawling shook a good-natured finger at me. "I don't remember anyone ever making it to stage five of that program. You have this gift, this talent, this—"

"You're about to lecture me, aren't you," I said, sighing. "You always start your lectures by giving me a compliment. Then you let me have it."

He laughed. "You've got me figured out. But I have to discuss your mistakes and what you can learn from them. If I don't, how will you be able to control the perfect virtual-reality robot?"

"That's another thing," I said. I was hot and thirsty. I was mad at the scientist who'd knocked me out with a rock.

I was grumpy. "Why do I need to control the perfect virtual-reality robot?"

Rawling gave me a strange look.

"I've been thinking about that a lot lately," I said, pressing forward. "I'm not the one who wants me to be perfect. *You* are."

Rawling still said nothing. I wondered if he was mad at me.

"Don't get me wrong," I responded quickly, "it's fun to become part of the program and pretend I'm actually outside of the dome. But I want the real thing. I want to get outside. I want to look up and actually see the sky and the sunset. Not just have it projected into my surround-sight helmet. I want—"

"Tyce," Rawling said quietly, "look down."

Even though I knew what was there, I looked down. At my wheelchair. At useless, crippled legs. At pants that never got ripped or torn or dirty because I was always sitting, legs motionless, in my wheelchair.

"I know, I know," I said sadly. "Sinking into Martian sand would eat up these wheels in less than a minute. But I can't let that stop me."

Rawling stared at me.

"You're the one," I murmured, "who always tells me this is only a handicap if I let it be a handicap."

Dome horns began to blare in short bursts. I counted. Four blares.

Four blares? That meant . . .

"A call for everyone to assemble," Rawling said, reading my mind.

Which meant the dome director was going to speak to all two hundred of us under the dome at the same time.

That hadn't happened since it looked like an asteroid might hit Mars, and that had been five years ago.

"I was afraid of this," Rawling muttered. He took my surround-sight helmet off my lap and set it beside the computer on the desk in front of me. "This may be your last computer run for a while."

"What?"

"It means a tekkie has confirmed my oxygen readings. Director Steven is going to tell all of us to avoid using electricity on anything except totally necessary activities. At least until we get our problem fixed."

"Oxygen readings? Problem fixed?"

This sounded serious. Too serious. Just as serious as the look on Rawling's face.

"Over the last week," he explained, "and during routine checkups, scientists and tekkies had complained to me about being too tired. And I've been tired myself."

Now that he mentioned it, my arms didn't feel that strong after pushing my wheelchair across the dome. And most of the time my arms were very strong, because I had to use them like my legs if I wanted my wheelchair to go anywhere.

"But I couldn't find anything wrong with them," he continued. "So without telling anyone, I took some oxygen readings. The dome was down 10 percent in oxygen levels."

"Ten percent!"

"That was three days ago," Rawling said. "I didn't want to spread panic, so I kept it to myself and asked the director to get a tekkie to confirm it. I hoped I was doing the readings wrong."

The dome horns began to blast again. Four blares.

Rawling waited until they finished. "I guess I wasn't

wrong. Worse, today my own readings showed we are now down 12 percent. Somehow the oxygen generators are failing little by little, and it looks like the problem is getting worse."

CHAPTER 3

With time running out, Mom wants me, Tyce
Sanders, to write all that is happening in a diary for
people to read on Earth when we are gone. We'll
store it on a hard drive here and have it sent by
satellite E-mail to the Internet systems of Earth
schools. That way kids who have been following
the Mars Project will get a chance to know about
our last days. She thinks it will mean more to
people coming from a kid my age than from any
scientist.

But I hardly know where to begin.

I mean, earlier this afternoon, my biggest worry
was whether I could conquer a virtual-reality
program where I controlled a super-robot. Now, the
oxygen level in the colony is dropping so fast that
all of us barely have five days to live.

I stopped and stared at my computer screen.

Writing is not easy for me. I used to think that because I
had a hard time with it, it meant I was dumb. Rawling
laughed one day when I told him that. He said I was not

dumb. He said most people found writing to be difficult. He said writing just took practice. He said sometimes adults forget that, and they expect their kids to be good writers instantly.

Hearing him say that made me feel better. And it made sense. It was unfair when adults looked at a kid's writing and expected that kid to be as good at it as adults who have been writing for years and years. So now I'm not as afraid to try to put my thoughts onto a computer screen.

I began to type again on the keyboard in my lap.

First, today's date. 06.20. 2039 A.D. Earth calendar. It's been a little more than fourteen years since the dome was established in 2025. When I think about it, that means some of the scientists and tekkies in the dome were my age around the year 2000, even though the last millennium seems like ancient history. Of course, kids back then didn't have to deal with water shortage wars and one-world governments and an exploding population that meant we had to find a way to colonize Mars.

Things have become so desperate on Earth that already 500 billion dollars has been spent on this project, which seems a lot, until you do the math and realize that's only about ten dollars for every person on the planet.

Kristy Sanders, my mom, used to be Kristy Wallace until she married my father, Chase Sanders. They teamed up with nearly two hundred men and women specialists from all countries across the world when the first ships left Earth. I was just a baby, so I can't say I remember, but

from what I've been told, those first few years of
assembling the dome were heroic. Of course, now
we live in comfort. I've got a computer that lets me
download e-entertainment from Earth by satellite,
and the gardens that were planted when I was a
kid make parts of the dome seem like a tropical
garden.

It isn't a bad place to live.

But now it could become a bad place to die.

Today Blaine Steven, the dome director, called
everyone together and told us that the gigantic
solar panels that covered most of the ceiling of the
dome are failing to make enough electricity to run
the dome and provide all our oxygen. He said if we
cut back our use of electricity to only what is absolutely needed, we can use the rest of the electricity
to make more oxygen. He warned that this alone
would not be enough. But the reserve oxygen in
the dome's spare tanks will get us through the last
few days until the supply ship arrives.

So no extra electricity can be used on anything.
The only reason I'm able to use my computer is
because it's running on battery. It means we won't
even use electricity for running showers. It's better
to be smelly and able to smell the smelliness,
Director Steven said, than to be clean and dead.
Everyone agreed.

Director Steven also said that most work under
the dome would be shut down. He said people
should rest and sleep and read books as much as
possible because resting bodies use less oxygen.
He said if all of us joined together we had a really
good chance of surviving.

Let me say this to anyone on Earth who might read this. If, like me, you have legs that don't work, Mars, with its lower gravity pull, is probably a better place to be than Earth.

That's only a guess, of course, because I haven't had the chance to compare Mars' gravity to Earth's gravity. In fact, I'm the only person in the entire history of mankind who has never been on Earth.

I'm not kidding.

You see, I'm the first person born on Mars. Everyone else here came from Earth nearly eight Martian years ago—fifteen Earth years to you—as part of the first expedition to set up a colony. The trip took eight months, and during this voyage my mother and father fell in love. Mom is a leading plant biologist. Dad is a space pilot. They were the first couple to be married on Mars. And the last, for now. They loved each other so much that they married by exchanging their vows over radio-phone with a preacher on Earth. When I was born half a Mars year later—which now makes me fourteen Earth years old—it made things so complicated on the colony that it was decided there would be no more marriages and babies until the colony was better established.

I stopped again. Because Mom tells me that much of the Mars Project has been explained so often in the media and in schools, I knew I didn't have to go into detail about the colony itself. I guessed everybody on Earth already knew that Phase 1 was to establish the dome. Phase 2, which we were just about to start, was to grow plants outside the dome so that more oxygen could be added to the atmosphere. The long-range plan—which would take over a hundred years—was to make the entire planet a place for humans to live outside of the dome.

People on Earth desperately needed the room. Already the planet had too many people on it. If Mars could be made a new colony, then Earth could start shipping people here to live. If not, new wars might begin and millions and millions of people would die from war or starvation or disease.

I wondered, though, if people really understood how different it was to live under a dome nearly fifty million miles away from the planet Earth.

I turned back to my keyboard.

What was complicated about a baby on Mars?

Let me put it this way. Because of planetary orbits, spaceships can only reach Mars every three years. (Only four ships have arrived since I was born.) And for what it costs to send a ship from Earth, cargo space is expensive. Very, very expensive. Diapers, baby bottles, cribs, and carriages are not exactly a priority for interplanetary travel.

I did without all that stuff. In fact, my wheelchair isn't even motorized, because every extra pound of cargo costs something like ten thousand dollars.

Just like I did without a modern hospital when I was born. So when my spinal column twisted funny during birth and damaged the nerves to my legs, there was no one to fix them. Which is why I'm in a wheelchair.

It could be worse, of course. On Earth, I'd weigh 110 pounds. Here, I'm only 42 pounds, so I don't have to fight gravity nearly as hard as Earth kids.

I thought about my father. I was growing tall, just like he was. Mom would often point to his photo and comment that I was also beginning to look like him. I had dark blond hair like he did. My nose and jaws and forehead were bigger than I wanted them to be, and I hoped the rest of my face would catch up so I would look more like him. I also knew he was big, like a football player. I would be heavier and bigger too if my legs didn't weigh next to nothing.

I hardly felt like I knew my father or he knew me because he didn't stay long between trips to Earth and back. For a long time I was always angry when I thought about this, because, from what I've read, most kids get to grow up with their fathers. And most kids get to grow up using their legs. But I've decided not to waste time caring about him or about what has happened to my legs.

I tapped at my keyboard, slowly putting more words together.

When my body and arms aren't weak from lack of oxygen, the lower gravity does make it easy to get around in my wheelchair.

The other good thing is that I never have to travel far. Not like on Earth, where you can go in one direction for thousands of miles. Here, all two hundred of us—mainly scientists and tekkies, the name we give technicians—live under a sealed dome that might cover four football fields. (I know all of this about Earth because of the DVD-gigarom books I scan for hours every day.)

When I'm not being taught by my computer or Rawling McTigre, I spend my time wheeling around the paths beneath the colony dome. I know every scientist and tekkie by first name. I know every path past every mini-dome, the small, dark plastic huts where people live in privacy from the others. Between the solar panels that crowd the ceiling I've seen every color of Martian sky through the super-clear plastic of the main dome above us. I've spent hours listening to sandstorms rattle over us. I've . . .

. . . I've got to go. Mom's calling for me to join her for meal-time.

I hit the save button on my keyboard. There would be plenty of time later to report more on our oxygen crisis, millions of miles away from rescue.

CHAPTER 4

Our mini-dome, like everyone else's, had two office-bedrooms with a common living space in the middle. Mom wasn't able to use her second room as an office because that had become my bedroom. We didn't need a kitchen, because we never had anything to cook. Instead, a micro-wave oven hung on the far wall; it was used to heat nutrient-tubes. Another door at the back of the living space led to a small bathroom. It wasn't much. From what I've read about Earth homes, our mini-dome had less space in it than two average bedrooms. And I could only dream about having a backyard and fence and garden the way I'd seen in e-photos.

Mom was waiting for me in one of the chairs in the common area. She had thick dark hair that was cut short, like an upside-down bowl. She didn't care much what she looked like—especially during the long, long months while my father was gone between refueling stops on Mars. It meant more to have a hairstyle that didn't take much fuss-ing and gave her as much time as possible for her science.

As the leading plant biologist on the station, Mom had a

big job: to genetically alter Earth plants so they could grow on Mars.

She gave me a tired smile—the fourteen-hours-of-hard-scientific-work smile. I gave her one in return.

"How are you doing with your diary?" she asked, like this was just another normal day.

"Fine," I said, like this was just another normal day. "What's for supper?"

Dying was funny. Not funny ha-ha. Funny strange. Everyone thought about it all the time, but nobody wanted to talk about it.

I grunted as I pushed my wheelchair toward her. It was getting harder and harder to move it. I worried that pretty soon I might not be able to move it at all.

Mom stood at the microwave and hit the buttons.

As I waited for the seconds to count down, I did what I always did whenever I had to wait.

I reached down to the pouch hanging from the armrest of my wheelchair and pulled out my three red juggling balls. I began to juggle, keeping all three in the air so that it looked like one blur. Some people twiddle their thumbs. Me, I like to juggle. Rawling says I learned it because it's something athletic I can do better than most people who aren't crippled. He's probably right.

The microwave dinged that it was ready.

I caught the juggling balls and put them in the pouch. With effort, I pushed my wheelchair toward Mom.

I finally reached her. She handed me a plastic nutrient-tube about the size of a chocolate bar. Red.

"Spaghetti and meatballs?" I asked.

She nodded. I've never tasted real spaghetti and meatballs, of course, so I have to take Mom's word for it that the nute-tube stuff is not nearly as good as the real thing.

As usual, she prayed over it.

As usual, I didn't.

As usual, it made her sad.

"Our oxygen level is dropping faster and faster," she said softly. "How can I convince you to place your faith in God? If we only have a month left . . . "

"I only believe what I can see or measure," I said. In the colony, I was surrounded by scientists. All their experiments were on data that could be seen—and measured.

"But faith is the confident hope in things unseen," Mom insisted, a bit teary-eyed. "Otherwise it wouldn't be a matter of faith. We don't see your dad, but we know he loves us, no matter where his cargo ship is. Faith in God is like that."

Right, I thought. I wasn't going to tell her that it wasn't easy to love a space-pilot father you never saw. And it wasn't easy to believe he loved me, either.

"Mom . . ." We had argued this so much that I decided to stick with the same old argument. "You can't make me believe in God. If you want me to pretend, I will."

"No," she said, with her mouth tight the way it is when she's vexed. "I always want you to be honest with me."

"There you go," I said. "End of argument."

I ripped off the top of my nute-tube. Most of the scientists needed to use a knife or scissors. I didn't. Because my legs were useless, I had developed a lot of strength in my arms and hands.

I guzzled the red paste, then tossed it on the table. "I'm going." Mom and I were good friends, but we were both grumpy from our argument about God and from the oxygen problem. I needed time by myself.

She didn't ask me where I was going. She didn't need to. There isn't much room in the dome for me to get lost.

And everyone knew I was a telescope freak. I spent any spare time I had on the third-level deck at the telescope.

By the time I wheeled to the center of the dome fifteen minutes later, I was sweating from the effort. Before, it only would have taken a couple of minutes and hardly any muscle power. This oxygen thing was scary. But what could I do about it?

The deck was dim because all but the most-needed lights had been shut down. Just another reminder of the oxygen problem.

Around me, men and women scientists walked slowly on the paths, going from mini-dome to mini-dome for whatever business they had. They nodded or said hello as they passed me.

In my wheelchair, I nodded and said hello back. Other than that, as I rolled along, I just stared upward at the stars above the dome. Other people on other expeditions might one day explore the planet outside. Not us. For starters, I wondered if we'd be dead soon. Dad was piloting the next cargo ship, and it wouldn't arrive for five days. One day after the colony dome ran out of oxygen.

I kept staring upward. My eyes drifted to the giant dark solar panels that hung just below the clear roof of the dome. These solar panels, which turned the energy of sunlight into electricity, were killing us. Part of this electricity powered our computers and other equipment. Most of the electricity, though, flowed as a current into the water of the oxygen tank. The electrical current broke the water—H_2O—into the gases of hydrogen and oxygen, two parts hydrogen for every one part of oxygen. The hydrogen was used as fuel for some of the generators. The oxygen, of course, we breathed.

But something was wrong with the panels. Nobody

could figure it out. Taken down and tested, they worked perfectly. But back up at the roof, the panels were making less and less electricity each day. With less power, we had less oxygen. It was that simple.

I focused upward, thinking about that.

Then it hit me.

It wasn't the panels. It was the sunlight.

What if the panels worked fine, but they weren't getting enough sunlight?

And I thought I knew why!

I spun my wheelchair around and began to move as fast as I could toward the director's mini-dome.

At that moment all of the dome's lights snapped off. The hum of the generator quit.

In total silence and darkness, I froze.

Then I heard a scream.

Unless I was wrong, that scream had come from the direction of my mini-dome.

CHAPTER 5

Within seconds, the total blackness inside the dome was filled with flashlight beams, making the air look like a giant confused sword fight of lights.

I still didn't move.

I didn't have a flashlight. I couldn't see where to go.

In a wheelchair, the last thing you want to do is hit something that will knock you flying. When you can't use your legs, it's embarrassing to have to crawl along the ground and try to pull yourself up into the wheelchair again.

More screaming reached my ears.

A strange blue glow began to appear in the dome, like neon ice melting in all directions.

The emergency backup lights were on.

In the glow, I saw a figure running toward me, with other figures chasing it.

"Hey!" I shouted.

Shouting was a very dumb thing to do. It alerted the running person to the fact that I was in my wheelchair and waiting.

Whoever it was turned sideways and shielded his face with his arm as he kept running toward me. In the weird glow of the blue emergency backup lights, I didn't have a chance of figuring out who it was.

He darted sideways to go around my wheelchair.

Sticking out my arm, I tried to stop him. Since people were chasing him, they probably had a reason for wanting to stop him.

That was another dumb thing to do. If I'd actually grabbed him, the force of his momentum could have ripped my arm off at my shoulder.

He passed me. Other dark figures got closer as they kept chasing him.

"Hey!" I shouted, louder. This time I did want to be seen. Getting trampled in my wheelchair is not my favorite evening activity.

"Hey!" I shouted one more time—and not because I wanted to warn anyone. This time it was because my wheelchair was suddenly moving.

The person behind me had given me a shove! He wanted me and my wheelchair to block the people chasing him.

I tried squeezing my brakes, but it was too late.

I was on one of the sidewalk paths between mini-domes. There was hardly any room to move around me on either side.

There must have been ten people chasing this guy. And with ten people all running like crazy, with hardly any room on the path to begin with, it's not fun to be the wheelchair that flies directly into the crowd.

Bang!

Something hard hit me in the face.

I tumbled out of my wheelchair and skidded on my chin into the side of a mini-dome. Two other people stepped on me and tripped. Someone behind them fell right on top of me. Then something else hard hit me on top of my head. Someone's knee, I found out later. It mashed my face into the floor of the dome. I cracked my forehead in a thump that sounded like wood against concrete.

After that, I didn't remember anything else, except that slowly it got darker and darker and the noises became quieter and quieter until I finally faded out completely.

CHAPTER 6

It smelled like someone was ramming a bottle of bleach up my nose.

Smelling salts.

It snapped me right out of my black daze.

I woke up with Rawling McTigre on one side of me, and my mother looking down, worried, from the other side. I was on my back on an examining table in the medical emergency room.

"Hey," I said with a croak. "Someone turned the lights back on."

Mom sighed with relief, smiled, and wiped my face with a cold wet cloth.

"Welcome back, scout," Rawling said. "Now you know what it would be like to play football."

"And be the football?" I groaned. "See, I told you it's a dumb game."

Rawling and I argue about that all the time. He's got a DVD-gigarom collection of Super Bowl games, and he loves watching them. I can't figure it out. A bunch of guys running into each other and a bunch more people screaming at them.

"What happened out there?" I asked. "I was just minding my own business when it went dark. I heard screams and then saw this guy getting chased and then—"

"He pushed you into the people chasing him and got away."

"Nobody gets away from anybody in this dome," I said. "It's too small."

"Whoever it was," Rawling replied, "got away long enough to stop running and find a way to mingle in with the crowds. That's the best way to hide in here. Just look like everybody else. He's not a stranger, of course, since the only humans on Mars are the ones already living under the dome."

Mom asked, "Did you get a look at his face?"

"Couldn't see anything," I said. "What did he do?"

"Nothing," Rawling said. "At least nothing we can figure out."

"I heard screaming and shouting in the dark."

"That came from the mini-dome next to ours," Mom said. "Someone pushed in one of the walls when the lights went out."

Not that collapsing a wall would be difficult. Although the mini-domes were built to act as temporary air-sealed shelters if the big dome ever temporarily lost its atmosphere, the walls were made of lightweight, rigid plastic.

"I don't get it," I said.

"Neither do we. The director, of course, has a security detail looking into it. Turn over."

"Huh?"

"You mean 'pardon me,' right?" Mom said, grinning at me.

"Yes, Mom," I said. "Pardon me?"

"Turn over," Rawling repeated. "I need to examine your back."

"It's my head that hurts," I said.

"Turn over," he insisted. "Doctor knows best."

Slowly I managed to flip myself over on the examining table. Although it would have been faster for Rawling to help me, he knew that was one thing I liked to do for myself.

Rawling lifted my shirt and ran his fingers up my back. He stopped near my neck and felt around.

"Does this hurt?" he asked.

"No."

He took his hands out from under my shirt and squeezed my neck, just above my shoulders. "Does this hurt?"

"No. I told you already. It's my head that hurts."

He moved my head gently from side to side. "Can you feel any pain in your neck when I do this?"

"Just my head."

"Good."

"Good? You like it that my head hurts?"

"Good that it doesn't appear you've done any damage to your back and shoulders. Come back tomorrow, and I'll take some X rays to be sure."

"Doc," I said, rolling over and sitting up, "why do you do this same exam of my back and shoulders every time I come in for a checkup?"

Seeming startled, Rawling glanced over at Mom. She looked quickly at me and then back at the doctor. She shook her head, as if she was telling him no.

"I worry about your spinal column," Rawling said. "It's not as strong as it should be."

He dropped his eyes.

Rawling never did that unless he was uncomfortable. I wondered if, for the first time, he was lying to me.

But I couldn't imagine why. And I couldn't imagine that Mom was in on the lie.

Things were getting weirder and weirder all the time.

CHAPTER 7

It's me again. Tyce. Remember, I was writing to all of you on Earth and got called away to supper. I'm back, but it's now the middle of the next day. Things got crazy here, and I didn't make it back to my computer right away like I planned.

Last night, I was going to tell you more about living under the dome.

Now it looks like all I have to write about is dying under the dome.

Last night, someone stole a bunch of reserve oxygen tanks. My friend and doctor, Rawling, says it took three people to do it. One person shut down the generator so the entire dome was dark. Another person pushed down a mini-dome and ran around in the dark with people chasing him. During this distraction, a third person used a trolley to take the reserve tanks.

I paused to rest my fingers. I thought about what I was writing.

The strangest part was that security had searched the

entire dome—think of exploring four football fields worth of gardens and mini-domes and small laboratory units—a dozen times and couldn't find those tanks. They are the size of scuba-diving tanks I've read about on my DVD-gigarom books. Except these tanks have super-compressed air and last ten people about two days each.

Twenty tanks were stolen. There should be no possible way for twenty tanks to be hidden. Not when the mini-domes are so small a person couldn't even hide one tank.

I wondered too about the three people who stole the tanks. As soon as they start to use the noisy tanks, they'll be found.

Unless they're going to wait until the rest of us are no longer breathing.

I wondered how they'd explain this when the spaceship finally arrived. My father and the other pilots would walk in and the people who stole the tanks would be the only ones healthy and living.

The latest newsflash: Director Steven now says that because of the stolen tanks, even if we don't use any electricity in the next three days, and even if all of us sleep all the time, we'll still run short of oxygen one day before the ship arrives.

I began to type again.

My friend Rawling told me this morning that some other people had a secret meeting. He was invited because he's a doctor. He was also invited because if Rawling agrees to something, most other people in the dome will agree. They trust him.

Well, the meeting is no longer a secret. Rawling got very angry with what they suggested. He not only refused to join them, he brought their idea immediately to the attention of Director Steven and wants them arrested.

You see, the people in this meeting did some math. They say that even after the oxygen tanks were stolen, there is enough oxygen under the dome for 180 people to survive until the ship arrives.

This means the dome needs twenty fewer people in it than it has now.

The people in this meeting want to draw names to see which twenty people should die.

CHAPTER 8

"Tyce, as you can imagine, I have very little time for anything else but the oxygen problem," Director Steven said. "As it is, I can only fit five minutes into my schedule for you. I hope this meeting is as important as you insisted."

Short and wide, Director Steven has thick, wavy, gray hair. He likes to run his hands through it as he talks. I think he does that because he likes to remind himself that he has way more hair than most people his age. He's over sixty, and a lot of the forty- and fifty-year-old scientists are going bald.

"Yes, sir," I said. I stayed very polite, even though I'd been asking to see him all day. The more I'd thought about my theory, the more I knew I was right. All of the oxygen problems could be solved. "I think I might know what's wrong with the solar panels."

Behind his desk, Director Steven leaned back in his chair. His office is the size of most entire mini-domes. He also has framed paintings of Earth scenes, like sunsets and mountains, on his wall. No one else has paintings. Cargo's too expensive.

"So tell me, *young* Tyce, what do you know that all our experts here don't know?"

By his tone of voice, I knew right then that I should have had Rawling bring my idea to Director Steven.

Rawling once told me that some people didn't like me simply because my unexpected birth here had taken time and resources that weren't planned. Rawling had explained that Director Steven was one of those people, especially because he acted like the entire Mars Project was his. The trouble was, this far from Earth, with him as commander, it basically was his project. So everybody had to do what he said.

"Sir," I began to explain. Now that I was here, it was too late to turn around. "I don't think the problem is with the solar panels."

"I see," he said sarcastically, running his fingers through his hair. "So it's just our imagination that the dome is running out of oxygen."

It wasn't fair that he treated me like I was just a stupid kid, not when I'd been forced to think and act like all the adults around me for as long as I could remember. If any of the adults in the dome had come in, Director Steven at least would have listened to them with respect. But I knew I couldn't say this, of course, or he'd get mad and tell me to leave. My point was too important.

"What I mean," I said as firmly as I could, "is that the tekkies have taken the solar panels down twice from the railings and found absolutely nothing wrong with them."

"Thank you, young Tyce, for telling me something I already know," Director Steven said mockingly. "You now have three minutes of my time left."

I tried to keep a polite smile on my face.

"If it's not the panels that are broken in some way," I said, "maybe then the problem is the sunlight."

"This is good," he said, leaning forward again. "Very good."

"It is?"

"You have been kind enough to help me understand this completely." He shook his head in disgust. "Now I've discovered we have to fix the sun."

"Sir, that's not what I mean. What if there is something blocking the panels from getting the sun?"

"Clouds? On Mars? Hardly. There's no atmosphere. Although that's our goal, we still haven't even found plants that will survive out there long enough to begin to create an atmosphere."

"What about the dome itself?" I asked. "In my virtual-reality computer sessions, the protective visors get scratched because of sandstorms. Maybe over the years Martian sand has done that to the dome, and less sunlight is getting through."

Director Steven stood abruptly and strode out from behind his desk. In his white lab coat, he appeared even larger than he was. From my wheelchair, I had to lean my head back to look up at him. I hated doing that because it made me feel small—and weak.

"Do you think we are stupid?" he thundered, looming over me. "Do you think when we designed this project we didn't think of that? The glass of the dome is as hard as diamonds. It was made to withstand the impact of small asteroids. A million years from now, the glass will still be as clear as the day it was made."

"I . . . I . . . was only trying to help," I said.

"You think you know all the answers," he said, his face red and furious. "Instead, you know nothing."

He leaned down in front of me and stared closely into my face.

"Dr. McTigre keeps me informed of your progress in the virtual-reality program, you know. He told me how you failed yesterday. How the scientist attacked you instead of letting you lead all of them across the plains in a sandstorm. And let me tell you why. It's because you didn't bother to explain how you could do it. You just assumed if you told them something, that's the way it was and they should listen. You should have learned yesterday that that technique doesn't work—before you wasted my time today. You're supposed to be smarter than that. Or are you?"

I kept my head as steady as I could. I knew nothing I could say would make a difference. I should have known better than to try to talk to Director Steven on my own. I should have remembered that he'd made it clear on numerous occasions that he couldn't be bothered by me—and that my presence alone under the dome had already bothered him enough over the years.

Director Steven's cold blue eyes bored into mine.

"Now please leave," he said flatly. "I have better things to do than let some teenager tell me how to run my project."

I went. Slowly. My wheelchair seemed like it was glued in place. Were my arms that dead already from lack of oxygen?

I'm not sure if I cared. My ears burned from anger and embarrassment.

Why did Director Steven seem to bristle every time he saw me? Did he dislike me that much? And if so, why? Was there something wrong with me?

CHAPTER 9

That night, after a very quiet and short supper, I decided to go up to the third deck, where the telescope was, because I wanted to be alone.

It was getting more difficult to push my wheelchair, and I needed to stop for breath a couple times. Each gasp I took reminded me of how little time was left before the oxygen ran out.

I wondered if I was breaking the new rule about resting to save oxygen. No one was jogging on the walkway. Below me, as I slowly wheeled up the catwalk, it was quiet on the main level of the dome. Most people were inside their mini-domes. But I decided that if I didn't have long to live, I didn't want to waste time I could spend with the telescope.

Tonight I not only wanted to take my mind off the oxygen problem, I wanted to forget what Director Steven had said to me.

Maybe I did think I was too smart. Maybe I did bug people.

Wondering about all that, and thinking about how useless and young he thought I was, I didn't like myself much either.

The best way to escape the dome and to escape myself was with the telescope on the third level. Because if my crippled body wasn't able to take me places, at least my eyes and mind and imagination could. For me, the telescope was freedom, something that let me travel a billion miles across the universe with a single sweep across the sky.

I rolled into place at the eyepiece of the telescope where the dome astronomer usually sat. I allowed myself a sad smile as I lifted my hands to the controls. The one good thing about useless legs was that you never needed to look for a chair.

I let out a deep breath as I reached the telescope controls.

The power to the computer controls of the telescope was down as part of the director's energy-saving program, but I knew how to find different stars and planets without the computer map. After all, the solar system was my backyard.

I brought the telescope into focus. The black of the universe and the brightness of the millions and millions of stars hit me with incredible clearness. It was a clearness no one would ever see on Earth, where the air and the clouds and the particles of pollution take away the sharpness of telescopes. But not on Mars, which has nearly no atmosphere. When you sit at the telescope, it feels like you can reach out and grab the stars.

In the next thirty seconds, Terror and Panic passed by me.

To anyone under the dome, that was an old, old joke. The names of the two moons of Mars are *Deimos* and *Phobos.* These Greek names translate to "terror" and "panic," because Mars was named after an ancient god of war.

But don't think of these moons like the one that circles Earth. Deimos and Phobos are tiny moons, chunks of rock not even twenty miles across. They are lumpy, not round, and they look like potatoes with craters. To us on Mars, Deimos rises in the east and sets in the west. Phobos rises in the west and sets in the east. They move across the sky in opposite directions. I never got tired of watching one moon pass by the other.

Tonight, though, I wasn't on the telescope deck to moon-watch. I wanted to see the planet Earth.

I turned the controls and fine-tuned the focus.

And there it was.

A beautiful blue ball, streaked with swirling white as storms crossed the face of it. And behind it, the round white moon, bouncing the sunlight and redirecting here to Mars.

I smiled sadly again.

The two hundred of us here on Mars were so far away. So alone in the vast solar system. To me, the Earth of DVD-gigaroms seemed so foreign, but nice—a place of people laughing and crying and falling in love and having picnics in parks and watching the sunset behind mountains and crossing oceans and flying through the air on jet planes.

Because of the oxygen problem, I'd never have a chance to see any of that. Or any of the other incredible things about living on a planet that Mom says God designed to make the existence of humans possible.

I blinked and went back to the telescope. Thinking about what I'd never see, I wanted to cry.

But I wouldn't allow myself to do it.

Because out of the two hundred people under this dome, I was the only kid, and used to being alone. I'd learned early not to cry, even when I felt like it. I'd learned early that, other than my mom and Rawling, I'd have to fend for myself. Nobody else in the colony paid much attention to me.

I stared at the Earth and the moon, hanging in the black

of a universe that was so big no human mind could truly understand its size.

I sat there a long time, thinking and wondering and feeling sad thoughts.

Then someone tapped on my shoulder.

It scared me so badly, I would have jumped out of my wheelchair if my legs had worked.

"Relax, Tyce," Rawling McTigre said. "It's only me. I thought I'd find you here."

"Yeah," I said, my heart still pounding. "You did."

"Look," he said in a strange tone. "We've got to talk. It's about a secret your mom and I have kept from you for a long, long time."

CHAPTER 10

Below us, it was dim. Shadows darkened the rows and rows of plants. The mini-domes looked like black eggs rising from the ground. Only the hum of the electrical generators broke the silence. And too soon, when all the electricity died, there would be no noise at all.

"Outside the dome," Rawling started to say in a low voice. He had pulled a chair near the telescope, and sat in it facing me directly so that our eyes were at the same height. "What does it take for a human to survive outside the dome?"

"I thought you were going to tell me a—"

"Outside the dome," he said again. "What does it take for a human to survive?" He spoke firmly, like he was quizzing me and wasn't going to say another thing until I answered.

"With or without a covered platform buggy?" I asked. The Mars Project has two of them. These monstrous machines ride on huge rubber tires that don't sink in the Martian sand because gravity is less here than on Earth.

I've seen photos of cars on Earth, and the platform buggies look nothing like them. They are simply four wheels that support a deck. On the bottom of the deck are the electric engine and storage compartments. On the top is a miniature dome, similar in shape to an Earth igloo, that covers the driver and passenger and can hold up to ten people. A small tunnel sticks out from the mini-dome onto an open portion of the deck where a ladder almost reaches the ground. This tunnel has two entrances to allow people to get in and out of the platform buggy when it's on the surface of Mars. The outside entrance is sealed as someone steps from the inner entrance into the tunnel. Then the inner entrance is sealed before the outer entrance opens. In this way, little oxygen escapes the platform buggy's mini-dome. The big entrance of the space station's dome works this way too.

"Without," he said. "You know how expensive the platform buggies are. They take a lot of room in cargo, cost millions to produce, and consume too much valuable energy when we run them. What does it take for a human to survive outside the dome without a platform buggy?"

"Humans need oxygen and water and protection from heat and cold."

"And how do they get all that now?"

"Big bulky space suits," I said. "And whatever oxygen and water each person can carry."

He asked, "How long can a human last out there until he or she needs to return to the dome?"

"Supposedly a day," I said. "Only a day. But that's why we're here. To get the planet ready for humans to live outside the dome. So that later—"

"Later is a hundred or two hundred years away. Meanwhile, the entire planet needs to be explored."

"Rawling, do you really have a secret? Or are you doing this to me to keep me interested?"

He didn't smile. "Machines. Robots. They don't need oxygen or water or heat. They don't take up a lot of cargo space on ships. For the cost of one platform buggy, you can have a hundred robots. Robots are ideal, except for one thing." He paused. "Robots don't have human brains. A computer as big as a spaceship can't think and react the way a human can. So we can't begin to send robots out to explore the planet unless they are controlled by, and think like, humans. . . . Are you with me so far?"

"Yes, but it hasn't been much of a secret. You said—"

"Tell me what you know about Earth labs that grow skin and bone for people."

"What does this have to do with—"

"Tell me."

"Sure, I'll tell you," I said. "You and Mom made me study it as part of a school assignment."

"So you understand that fifty years ago, burn victims had no chance of healing their skin. But now doctors can take a piece of the victim's skin and grow it into big patches, just like growing a plant, then replace the damaged skin with the new skin."

"Yes, I know. Remember? You made me study it for three months as—"

"And you know about replacement bones and replacement organs and how far that has come since the year 2000. And that doctors have learned how to grow biological plastics right inside the body. They have used steel and cable to rebuild joints. They've found ways to join all sorts of artificial materials to human body parts."

"Yes, yes, yes," I said, trying hard not to get impatient. "Come on, Rawling. What's the secret?"

"Put it together," he said, slowly and quietly. "The need for robots with human brains, along with advances in medicine. Add one more thing, then you'll have your secret."

CHAPTER 11

"One more thing," I repeated. "I don't get it."

"Virtual reality," Rawling said. "You've been in that robot simulation program two hours a day since you were eight years old. Tell me what you know about virtual reality."

"Well," I started slowly, "I put on the surround-sight helmet. It gives me a three-dimensional view of a scene on a computer program. The helmet is wired so that when I turn my head, it directs the computer program to shift the scene as if I were there in real life. Or in the case of the robot training, it shifts to whatever video lens I want, giving me the chance to see in four directions, one direction at a time."

"Go on," he said.

"Sounds come in like real sounds. Because I'm wearing a wired jacket and gloves, the arms and hands I see in my surround-sight picture move wherever I move my own arms and hands."

"Good," he said.

"Good? I'll bet any five-year-old Earth kid knows this stuff. What about this secr—"

"Will you agree with me that the virtual-reality helmet and jacket are just extensions for your brain?"

He must have seen my puzzled look.

He pointed at the telescope. "Just like this is an extension of your brain. You can't actually be on a moon of Jupiter, but the telescope lets your eyes go there, and your eyes show the moon to your brain."

"That's different," I said. "A moon of Jupiter is real. Virtual reality is just a computer program."

"Your brain doesn't know the difference. Not unless you tell your brain with your thoughts."

"Rawling," I said, "if you're trying to confuse me, it's working."

"Stick with me," he said. "This is important. Does your brain see?"

I thought about it. "No. My eyes see."

"You got it. Your eyes deliver information to your brain. When you look through the telescope, your optic nerves take the image and fire it into your brain. Your brain translates the information. But your brain doesn't see. It relies on the extensions of the brain. Your eyes. Your telescope. Or the extension of virtual reality."

I was beginning to understand.

"Your brain doesn't see anything," he said. "It doesn't hear anything. It doesn't smell anything. It doesn't taste anything. It doesn't feel anything. Your brain is this incredible jumble of stuff packed into your skull that translates the information delivered to it by nerve endings. Some nerve endings are attached to the back of your eyes. Or to your ear canals. To sensors in your nose or on your tongue. To nerve endings in your skin and bones."

"In other words," I said, "you are telling me the body is like a virtual-reality suit wrapped around the brain."

"Exactly!" He smiled. "After all, it's like God designed an amazing twenty-four-hour-a-day virtual-reality suit that moves on two legs, has two arms to pick things up, can feed and repair itself, and is equipped to give information through all five senses. Except instead of taking you through virtual reality, a made-up world, your body takes you through the real world."

"I'd never thought of it that way," I said. "But I'll agree with you. Now will you finally tell me the secret?"

"Soon," he said. "But give me one more minute."

"One minute."

"It takes time for the brain to learn how to handle all the information delivered by the body," he said, excitedly falling into the teacher role. "For proof, all you need to do is watch a baby as it grows. Babies are clumsy and don't know how to work their bodies. Or how to understand the sights and sounds that their eyes and ears deliver to their new brains. But slowly, their brains figure out what information is being delivered, and babies begin to understand the world around them through the nerves of their eyes and ears and nose and tongue and skin."

"I know, I know," I said. "For my first two years in controlling a virtual-reality robot in the computer program, you always laughed and said that except for smelly diapers, I was just like a newborn baby."

"Because you were like a newborn," he said in a serious tone. "Your brain was learning to translate new information. Only this new information didn't come from your body, but from the virtual-reality equipment, which was just like the extension of your body. You were clumsy at first, but quickly you got better until you now handle that virtual-reality robot just as if it were your own body. Learning those controls was like learning the controls of a complicated computer game."

He took a deep breath. "So you're still with me after all that?"

"Yes."

He took another deep breath. "Let me ask you this. If the information was delivered instantly, would it make a difference to your brain if the information reached it through eyes attached to your head, or eyes attached to a video lens a thousand miles or a million miles away?"

"It would," I said, after thinking about it for a few seconds. "Because your hands have to be near your eyes to pick something up."

"What if your hands were also a thousand miles or a million miles away?"

"Ha, ha," I said. "I know your secret. You're crazy. Like anybody could have arms a million miles long."

"I'm serious," he said. "It's the brain that matters, and how it deals with the information. If your eyes and ears and hands are just extensions of your brain, it doesn't matter how far away all those parts are, as long as two things are possible. First, these extensions instantly deliver information to the brain. And second, the brain is instantly able to direct the extensions. Will you agree with me?"

I looked at Rawling strangely. He was waiting as if my answer was very important.

"Well," I said. "I guess you're right. It wouldn't matter."

"If it doesn't matter, Tyce, you could explore Mars. You could go out to the asteroids. You could see a moon of Jupiter. Not by telescope, but by actually being there through extensions of your eyes and ears and the rest of your senses in the body of a robot. Would you like that?"

"You know I hate this wheelchair," I said. "But what you're talking about, that can't happen. It's only theory."

Rawling looked up through the dome at the stars. Then back at me.

"It's no longer theory," he said softly. "It's you."

CHAPTER 12

"I promised your mother I wouldn't say anything else until we got together with her," Rawling said as he got up out of his chair. "She's waiting for us in your mini-dome."

"You can't leave me hanging like this. . . . "

"It won't be long," he said. "Let me get you down there."

Normally, I didn't let anyone push my wheelchair. I mean, did other people ask for help when they walked? This time, though, I was too distracted, wondering about what Rawling had just told me.

Rawling wheeled me away from the telescope and took us down the catwalk to the second level. As he pushed me along the second level walkway, he grunted.

"You must be getting heavier," he said. "I don't ever remember it being this difficult to move you around."

"Lack of oxygen," I said. "It's been getting tougher and tougher for me to wheel around, too."

But now I didn't care about that. I wanted to know more about the virtual-reality program. "Will you at least give me a hint about this robot stuff?"

"You won't have to wait long. Trust me, for as long as

this secret has been inside you, another few minutes won't matter."

"Inside me?"

"Inside you. But I won't say another word until we meet your mother."

He kept pushing. When we reached the ramp, he guided me down to the main level. In another couple of minutes, we met my mother in our mini-dome.

"An X ray," Rawling said as he handed me a big envelope. "An X ray of your back and shoulders. From this afternoon's checkup."

I glanced up at him.

He sat in one chair on the other side of the mini-dome's common area. Mom sat on another.

"First of all," Rawling began, "you should know that we weren't going to tell you this until you were eighteen, the age of legal adulthood on Earth. A long time ago it was decided that when you reached that age, you would be given the choice to go ahead with the experiment or not. Except now, with the dome losing oxygen . . . "

He didn't have to finish for me. What he meant was that I wouldn't reach my eighteenth birthday.

"Anyway," he said, "look at the X ray."

I did, opening the envelope and holding the sheet up to the light.

The bones were gray-white against the darker film of the X-ray sheet. I could easily see the collar bones and shoulder blades and the top of my spinal column and the bottom of my skull.

"See where your neck is?" Rawling asked. "You'll have

to look closely. See that short, dark rod, hardly thicker than a needle?"

I squinted at the X ray and finally nodded. It was wedged directly into my spinal column, at the bottom of my neck, just above the top of my shoulder blades. It looked like thousands of tiny hairs stuck out of the end of the needle into the middle of my spinal column.

"That's been there since you were a year old," Rawling said.

"What is it?" I asked. "How did it get there?"

Mom spoke very quietly. "It got there as part of an operation. I agreed to let them attach it to your spine. It was a very difficult decision, one I struggled with making. But in the end, I felt I had no choice. I hope you will forgive me."

"Forgive you? But . . . "

"Tyce, it made things very hard here at the dome when we discovered I was going to have a baby. Everything for this project had been planned down to the last detail. You weren't one of those details. Director Steven was furious. But he couldn't send me back. They needed a plant biologist too badly to begin experimental work on hybrids for Mars. If I went back to Earth, with the time it takes to travel back and forth, it would put them years behind as they waited for a replacement. Director Steven threatened to send you back instead, as soon as you were born. But I knew the journey in a spaceship would kill you. Babies can't handle the stresses of g-force and orbit shifts. So when he offered me a trade, I accepted it." Her eyes lowered to her hands.

"A trade?"

"Remember," she said, "I loved you too much to send you away and risk your death."

"A trade?" I asked again.

Mom hesitated. "Director Steven said everyone on the dome project needed to have a purpose," she finally answered, her eyes staring straight at me as if judging my reaction to her news. "Including you. So I agreed to the operation on your spine. The next ship brought in a neurosurgeon and all the experimental equipment needed. After the operation, the neurosurgeon went out on the next flight. He was paid six years' salary for all the time he spent in travel. But no one cared about the money, because it was decided that you could be the one to revolutionize space exploration."

"Me?" I said.

"As part of the long-term plan," Rawling said, "scientists had been hoping to use robots to explore Mars and do work that humans couldn't, based on virtual-reality extensions. The next stage in their experiments was to hook up the human nervous system directly into a robot's computer drive. They were hoping a human brain could control the robot."

In a flash, I understood why Rawling had always examined my back so closely during checkups. Why he'd been worried about my back after I fell out of the wheelchair the night before. Why he'd spent two hours a day since I was eight Earth years old, training me in the virtual-reality robot program. Why Mom and Rawling had made me learn everything possible about human implants.

"The needle in my back," I queried, holding up the X ray against the light. "All those things at the end of the needle that look like fine hairs. Those are biological implants that have grown into my nerves."

Mom and Rawling nodded.

"Plastic fibers with a core that transmits tiny impulses of electricity," Rawling said. "You are the first person to get this implant. They hadn't planned on trying it in a human on Mars for at least another ten years."

"Wow!" I couldn't keep excitement out of my voice. If I was right . . .

"And the end of the needle coming out of my spinal column," I said, "it will attach directly to a computer input, right?"

Again they nodded.

"It will take a painless minor operation to cut open the skin and add an antenna plug to the needle," Rawling said. "It will barely stick out of your back."

"Double wow!" I said. Now everything Rawling had just talked about at the telescope made sense. The need for robots powered by human brains. Medical advances over the last fifty years. Virtual-reality extensions of the human brain. "You mean I can be hooked up to a robot?"

"If it works," Rawling said flatly. But he didn't seem happy. "Remember, no one has tried this before."

My mind raced. *The senses of the robot will be an extension of my body! Just by using my brain, I'll be able to travel without my wheelchair! I'm going to be the one to revolutionize space exploration! The places I can go in a robot's body are limitless. I can . . .*

Tears rolled down Mom's face.

"I don't get it," I said, puzzled. "This is great news. What's there to forgive you for?"

Mom didn't wipe away the tears.

"Tyce," she said slowly, "I've lied to you about one thing since you were old enough to talk . . . and it has pained me to do so. I have agonized over my decision ever since, wondering if I made the right one—letting my baby become an experiment. So here's the truth . . . you didn't lose the use of your legs because of the way you were born."

I stared at her. I didn't understand.

"It happened during the operation," she finished. "When the neurosurgeon inserted the rod into your spine, he accidentally cut some of the nerves that go to your legs."

CHAPTER 13

When Mom asked me to write this Mars diary, I thought it was going to be about living and dying under the dome. Instead, it has become learning about myself.

First of all, I'm scared. And it's been that way ever since two days ago, when I learned the truth about my handicap. At first I was excited about the thought of zooming around in a robot's body. But then reality settled in. This afternoon I'm going to be hooked up to the computer drive of a robot through the nerves of my spinal column. Rawling says it should work, but no one has ever tried it before. He says something might go wrong. It could do something to my brain if the electrical circuits haven't fused properly to my body with the biological plastic connections.

I say, what does it matter since I might die anyway from the oxygen problem in this dome?

I've also learned I'm crippled not from birth, as I've thought all these years, but because an experimental operation went wrong when I was a baby.

I don't know whether to be mad or sad about this. Or happy that I've got a chance to do something in space that no other person in history has been able to try.

Either way, it won't change the fact that my legs are useless.

I stopped typing at the keyboard. I reached for my red juggling balls from my wheelchair pouch and tossed them in the air. My hands automatically juggled while my brain thought.

I needed to comfort myself with juggling because if I let myself think about what I didn't want to think about, I'd go crazy.

But here I was, beginning to think about what had made me cry all last night. I told myself to think about the operation that crippled me instead.

In a way, I felt more sorry for Mom than I did for myself. She's the one who feels guilty over what happened because of the operation, although it isn't her fault. She didn't have much of a choice: Either she had to send me off to certain death on the spaceship or allow me to stay and become part of an experimental procedure. And she'd only had a short time to make the decision—and all when my dad was out of communication range, so she had to make the choice on her own.

Maybe I should be mad at Director Steven, who forced Mom to make the choice. But he didn't plan on the operation going wrong.

It did explain, though, why he always seemed to dislike me. Now I knew I reminded him of his terrible mistake in forcing me to be an experiment without any choice. At least that's what Rawling says.

It wouldn't do much good to get mad at Director Steven anyway, since it wouldn't change my situation.

And I knew Director Steven had plenty of other problems now.

I stopped juggling and went back to writing.

Late the night I'd found out the real truth about my legs, one of the scientists went to Rawling with a committee's decisions—the committee Rawling had refused to join.

They call themselves the "Life Group." They now have seventy-five people, too many for security to arrest or fight. This means they now have enough power to rule the dome. They say that unless Director Steven agrees to help them, they will do it themselves. They are trying to force him to make sure that twenty people die early so that the other 180 will live. If Director Steven doesn't help them, they'll find a way to pick those twenty people themselves.

Then yesterday morning, Director Steven called another meeting for everyone under the dome. He said he didn't agree with the Life Group but was afraid a war would start if he didn't try to do something.

Director Steven said we had three days to figure out what was wrong with the generators. After that there would only be enough oxygen left for 180 people to survive until the ship arrived. He said at this point he felt he should see if any volunteers would give up their lives to help save the others if the generators did not get fixed.

It was very quiet when he asked for those volunteers.

I felt tears begin to roll down my cheeks again.

I mean, what would you do in the same situation? If you were going to die anyway when the oxygen was gone, would you volunteer to die early so that you could save others? Or would you hope that others volunteered to die early so you could be saved?

I wish I could tell you what I decided about volunteering. But I wasn't given a chance. So I'll never know for sure, no matter what I tell myself.

Director Steven said some people wouldn't be allowed to be volunteers because of what they contributed to the long-term project. I was one of those people. He had learned through Rawling that I'd said "yes" to the experiment where the nerves of my spinal column would be attached to a robot's computer drive.

I forced myself to write in my diary what happened next.

Altogether, there were about a hundred people who would be allowed to volunteer to save the others. When he asked again for twenty, nobody looked at anybody.

Then I heard a movement as some people stepped out of the back of the group.

Director Steven had asked for twenty volunteers, and three decided to give up their lives if the generator wasn't fixed in time.

I cried all last night. I haven't cried in years. But I couldn't help myself.

One of those volunteers was my mom.

CHAPTER 14

"Tyce, you know I'm a Christian. I believe God created humans with a body, a mind, and a soul. I know you can't prove the existence of a soul. You tell me that all the time. But you can't prove it doesn't exist, either."

Mom stood beside my wheelchair in the part of the dome that overlooked the ferns and trees planted in straight rows. She had a hand on my shoulder.

"You are correct. No scientific instrument will measure or prove the existence of God or the soul," she continued. "But no scientific instrument can prove the existence of love or loneliness either. But love exists. So does loneliness. You can feel it. And I believe your soul will be filled with one or the other."

"Please," I begged, "please change your mind about being one of the twenty."

I fought hard not to cry in front of her. It was bad enough when I did it alone.

"I know we've had these talks before," she stated. "But listen to me again. If we have souls—and the Bible says we do—then there is more to this life than what we see with our human eyes. And there is someone beyond, waiting: God, who created us and this universe."

"Mom . . ." I couldn't help it. I began to cry.

She squatted beside me and stared into my face. She smoothed my hair as she spoke. "Tyce," she continued, "I love you. I love you so much it breaks my heart to think of leaving you behind. But my faith would be worth nothing if I could not face death bravely because of it. Our human lives are just a blink in eternity compared to God's promise of where my soul will fly after it leaves my body."

"No . . . ," I blubbered. "You can't. I don't want you to leave me behind."

She spoke very quietly. "Tyce, I can't make you believe what I believe. But I hope that when you see how strongly I believe in God—even accepting death because of it—that my faith might lead you to believe in God, too. If my sacrifice brings you home to God, then it'll be worth it. And I've already asked Rawling to take care of you when your father isn't here."

"All right," I said, tasting the salt of my tears. "I'll believe. I'll believe. If that's what it takes to save you, I'll believe anything. Just tell Director Steven you've changed your mind."

She stood again and stared out at the plants. "You know I can't do that," she said. "But don't give up so fast. We still have two days to find a way to fix the generators."

CHAPTER 15

"Your upper back giving you much pain?" Rawling asked.

"No," I said. "Can't feel a thing."

We were in the computer lab room. I was on my back on a narrow medical bed in the computer laboratory. I wore a snug, navy-blue jumpsuit. My head was propped on a large pillow so that the plug at the bottom of my neck didn't press on the bed. This plug was wired to an antenna that was sewn into the jumpsuit. Across the room was a receiver that would transmit signals between the body suit antenna and the computer drive of the robot. It worked just like the remote control of a television set, with two differences. Television remotes used infrared and were limited in distance. This receiver used X-ray waves and had a hundred-mile range.

A half-hour earlier, Rawling had frozen the area of skin below my neck with a needle injection. It had taken Rawling less than five minutes to find the rod in my spine and attach a computer plug to the end of it. With the plug sticking out, Rawling had stitched the small opening of my skin around the plug with careful, tight loops, explaining that if we weren't so short on time, we'd have waited a week for the skin to heal.

I didn't care about a few stitches that I couldn't feel anyway. I wanted to get started as soon as possible to see if this would work. My wheelchair was empty in the corner, and I hoped to keep the wheelchair empty for as long as possible. I'd dreamed my whole life about walking, and if it took my brain and a robot's body to do it, I was ready.

"I've got to go over this one more time," Rawling said. "I can't tell you enough how important this is."

"No problem. I'm ready," I said.

"Tyce . . . ," Rawling warned.

"Um, ready to listen just one more time," I quickly finished.

"Good," Rawling said.

Rawling began pulling straps tight across my legs to hold me snugly to the bed.

"First," Rawling said, "it won't be good if you move and break the connection. I doubt it will happen, since only your brain will be responding, and your brain, of course, cannot move. But this will be the first time anyone has ever done this, and I'd rather be safe than sorry."

Rawling tightened down the straps across my stomach and chest.

"Second, don't allow the robot to have contact with any electrical sources. Ever. Your spinal nerves are attached to the plug. Any electrical current going into or through the robot will scramble the X-ray waves so badly that the signals reaching your brain may do serious damage."

Rawling placed a blindfold over my eyes and strapped my head in position. Immediately, it began to itch under my chin.

"Lastly," Rawling directed, "disengage instantly at the first warning of any damage to the robot's computer drive. Your brain circuits are working so closely with the computer circuits that any harm to the computer may spill over to harm your brain."

"Understood, understood, and understood," I said. I wanted to scratch myself under my chin. "I'm ready."

"No, you're not," Rawling answered. "Tell me how you're going to control the movements of the robot for me."

I spoke directly to the ceiling. My eyes were shut beneath the blindfold. "From all my years of training in a computer simulation program, my mind knows all the muscle moves I make to handle the virtual-reality controls. This is no different, except instead of actually moving my muscles, I imagine I'm moving the muscles. My brain will send the proper nerve impulses to the robot. It will move the way I made the robot move in the virtual-reality computer program."

"Correct," Rawling said, sounding pleased. "It may feel strange at first, sending brain impulses in this way. Don't panic if it takes you some time to figure this out. Now, tell me when and how you disengage your mind from the robot controls."

My chin was driving me crazy. "If I see any object about to strike the robot's computer drive or if I feel the robot begin to fall or otherwise get close to danger, in my mind I shout *Stop!* The combination of throat and neck muscle movement from my brain impulses, plus the sound of that one single word, triggers the computer drive to disengage me instantly, and my brain awareness returns to my body here on the bed."

"Excellent," Rawling said. "Remember, this afternoon is just a test run back and forth in this laboratory. Nothing fancy or dangerous. Right?"

"Right."

"You know the blindfold is here to protect your real eyes

from visual distractions. I also need to make sure your real ears can't hear anything. Any questions before I put the headphones over your ears?"

"Just one," I said.

"Yes?"

"Could you please, please scratch under my chin?"

CHAPTER 16

In motionless darkness and silence, I had no sense of time. I knew Rawling would need to download the virtual-reality program into the robot's computer drive. But I couldn't guess exactly when this might happen.

As I waited, I pictured the robot.

Its lower body was much like my wheelchair. Instead of a pair of legs, an axle connected two wheels. Just like a wheelchair, it turned by moving one wheel forward while the other remained motionless or moved backward.

I knew I could handle direction changes easily. After all, in my real body, the use of spinning wheels was the only way I'd ever moved through the dome.

The robot's upper body was a short, thick hollow pole that stuck through the axle, with a heavy weight to counter-balance the arms and head. Within this weight was the battery that powered the robot, with wires running up inside the hollow pole.

At the upper end of the pole was a crosspiece to which arms were attached. They were able to swing freely without hitting the wheels. Like the rest of the robot, the arms and hands were made of titanium and jointed like human arms, with one difference. All the joints swiveled. The hands, elbows, and shoulder joints of the robot could rotate in a full circle, as well as move up and down. The hands, too, were like human hands, but with only three fingers and a thumb instead of four fingers and a thumb.

Four video lenses at the top of the pole served as eyes. One faced forward, one backward, and one to each side.

Three tiny speakers, attached to the underside of the video lenses, played the role of ears, taking sound in. The fourth speaker, on the underside of the video lens that faced forward, produced sound. This was the speaker that would allow me to make my voice heard.

The computer drive of the robot was well protected within the hollow titanium pole that served as the robot's upper body. Since it was mounted on shock absorbers, the robot could fall ten feet without shaking the computer drive. This computer drive had a short antenna plug-in at the back of the pole, to give and take X-ray signals.

I felt my heart beating fast in suspense. When was it going to happen? When was the computer drive going to be ready? What would it be like? Would it work?

It seemed I waited forever in the darkness and silence of the blindfold and soundproof headphones.

I was just about to open my mouth and ask Rawling if there was a problem.

Then it happened.

I began to fall off a high, invisible cliff into a deep, invisible hole.

I kept falling and falling and falling. . . .

CHAPTER 17

"Tyce! Tyce! Tyce!"

In the blackness, my name echoed weirdly around me, as if I were trapped in a metal barrel.

"Tyce! Tyce! Tyce!" My name was so loud, it hurt.

I lifted my hands to my head to cover my ears. That movement seemed to rip the darkness off my eyes. I saw three pairs of titanium hands waving wildly, fuzzy and blurry.

"Not so loud," I complained.

Except my words came out slow and deep and warbly.

The three pairs of hands still waved wildly.

Then I realized I saw three pairs because I was using three eyes—the video lenses on each side and the forward lens.

I blinked a few times and concentrated straight ahead.

Much better. Now it was only one pair of wildly waving hands, fuzzy and blurry.

"Tyce!"

"Not so loud," I complained again in my robot voice.

I stared at my hands.

Oops. My video lens zoomed in too close. A giant titanium knuckle filled my view.

I zoomed back. I saw the wall and bed and my body strapped on the bed.

Weird!

My hands still waved. Finally I managed to get the focus right.

Then I asked myself why I was doing something dumb like watching my hands work. Was I a little baby who had never seen fingers work before?

I thought about dropping my hands to my side and letting them rest there. Instantly, they moved where I wanted.

This was great!

"Tyce!"

It was Rawling. He had moved directly in front of me. My front lens saw his stomach.

Up, I mentally commanded myself.

The video lens tilted up.

I saw his face looking down on me. Blinking a few times to focus better, I saw his nose hairs. Too close. I backed out a bit. Then it was just right.

"You're too loud!" I complained.

"It's not me," he said. "I'm whispering. You must be trying to hear too hard. Those speakers can pick up the sound of a feather landing on a floor. I'm turning them down."

I thought of listening less hard. The volume of his voice dropped.

This was very, very fun.

"Rawling," I said, focusing on speaking properly. My voice become more normal. "How are you?"

"This is unbelievable," he said excitedly. "It's you in there!"

I blocked out my front view and switched to a side lens. It showed my body on the bed again.

I zoomed in close. My chest rose and fell as the body breathed.

"Yes," I said, "it's me in here."

I kept watching the bed.

It was very strange. That was my body on the bed, but it wasn't my body. My brain was working, controlling a robot's body. Very, very strange.

I switched to the rear video lens, then the other side, and then the front again. In a fast blur, it showed the back wall, the side wall, and then Rawling's face.

Big mistake.

Going in a circle that fast made me dizzy. I wouldn't do that again.

"Can you move?" Rawling asked.

In my mind, I pictured shoving back in my wheelchair.

Both robot wheels responded instantly.

In a flash, I was going backward.

Too fast!

Without thinking, I switched to the rear video lens.

The back wall was approaching too quickly.

Stop, I commanded the wheels. *Stop!*

In that instant, I fell into blackness again. Off that high, invisible cliff into that deep, invisible hole.

Just like that, I was back in my body. I felt the straps against my stomach and chest. I felt my itchy chin.

And I heard a loud crash.

"Tyce!" Rawling shouted. "Are you all right?"

"Yeah," I said from the bed. I'd forgotten the stop command would disengage me from the computer drive. "But how's our robot?"

CHAPTER 18

Hello again, diary. I feel like a person in a cave who has just found enough gold to make him rich for the rest of his life, then watches as the cave entrance gets covered by a landslide. What good is the gold going to do then?

For me, the experiment with the robot was the best thing that happened to me. I had freedom for the first time in my life.

Rawling spent the rest of the afternoon with me. The robot wasn't damaged from smashing into the back wall, so we put it through dozens of trial runs. And each time I got a little better at using it. All the years in virtual-reality training have paid off for us.

I rested my fingers, thinking about what I'd write next in the diary.

The robot is amazing. It has heat sensors that detect infrared, so I can see in total darkness. The video lenses' telescoping is so powerful that I can recognize a person's face from five miles away. But I can also zoom in close on something nearby, and look at it as if using a microscope.

I can amplify hearing and pick up sounds at higher and lower levels than human hearing. The titanium has fibers wired into it that let me feel dust falling on it, if I want to concentrate on that miniscule of a level. It also lets me speak easily, just as if I were using a microphone.

It can't smell or taste, however. But one of the fingers is wired to perform material testing. All I need are a couple specks of the material, and this finger will heat up, burn the material, and analyze the contents.

It's strong, too. The titanium hands can grip a steel bar and bend it.

Did I mention it's fast? Those wheels will move three times faster than any human can sprint.

I described all of this in my diary and continued. . . .

I love this robot. I can hardly wait to get back into it tomorrow.

All of this is the good news, just like finding gold.

The bad news, of course, is that we are one day closer to the dome running short of oxygen.

I finally have my freedom. And now I might lose it.

But worse, way worse, is the scary thought that Mom has volunteered to leave the dome so that others can survive. I can't handle it. Life seems so unfair. I keep telling myself that somehow the solar panels will be fixed before tomorrow at noon.

Because that's when twenty people must get sent onto the surface of the planet to die.

CHAPTER 19

The next day, two hours before the deadline to have the solar panels fixed, Director Steven called another general meeting. It took me and Rawling away from our experiments with the robot.

All two hundred of us—director, dome tekkies, scientists, and me—met at the assembly area. I sat near the front, still in my wired jumpsuit, since I wouldn't be able to see over anyone in my wheelchair.

This assembly was different than the others.

Normally, Director Steven stood alone at the front, on a small platform, when he spoke.

This time, the dome's five security guards, armed with stun guns, stood beside him. The guards were big men, their muscles like slabs of rock beneath their jumpsuits. In all the years of the Project, they'd never been required to do actual police work. Today they looked very stern and serious.

Parked at the side were both of the dome's platform buggies. I fought tears since they were here for only one reason: To take my mom away.

She stood beside me. For once, I didn't care what other people thought. I reached out and held her hand.

"Please don't go," I said. "Please."

"I love you, Tyce." She spoke quietly, but there was a tear in her eye. "Never forget that. And remember that God loves you, too. You can trust him to be with you every minute, more than I can ever be. So you'll never be alone."

"Please don't—"

Director Steven began to speak, cutting me off. All the people behind me stopped their murmuring and shifting.

"I would say good morning," Director Steven said grimly, "but this is not a good morning. The final deadline approaches, and we've found no solution for the loss of oxygen. All seals to the dome have been checked. We're not leaking oxygen. We've taken apart the solar panels again and again, and we cannot determine why they fail to produce enough electricity to maintain oxygen levels. I now face the most difficult moment I've ever faced as Director of the Mars Project."

He stopped to draw a breath. "These platform buggies will take some of us away from the dome. All radio contact between the platform buggies and the dome will cease. Those on the platform buggies will not be coming back. They will be heroes, making possible not only the lives of those who remain, but moving the Mars Project forward. As you know, it's critical to keep the Mars Project on schedule, because each extra year it takes to get the planet ready is an extra year that millions will starve on an overpopulated Earth. Because of that, the few who leave today will not only save the 180 who remain behind, but the lives of millions of others. Those who leave on these platform buggies will be remembered for their sacrifice for as long as mankind exists."

He looked at Mom and smiled sadly, then addressed the rest of the crowd.

"As you know," he continued, "we've had a few volunteers agree to leave the dome. However, we'll need to remove at least twenty people for there to be enough oxygen for the others to survive until the ship arrives. For that reason, I've drawn names."

Immediate angry shouting rose like thunder around me.

Director Steven put up his arms in a request for quiet. It took several minutes.

He spoke again. His face appeared weary, unlike the cocky director who such a short time ago had insisted I leave his office. "Do any of you see another way? We cannot permit everyone to die. Better a few should die than all of us."

More shouting. Again he raised his arms. This time it took even longer for him to be able to speak.

"Understand two things. First, the security guards have been instructed to enforce this order. Their guns are set on stun. If your name is drawn, and you refuse to go, you'll be placed on the platform buggy by force. Please don't make this more difficult on all of us."

The shouting grew even louder and longer. Now it didn't make a difference that Director Steven held his hands high and pleaded for silence.

Finally he stepped down from the platform and headed toward one of the platform buggies. In the roar of the shouting, he climbed the buggy's ladder. When he reached the deck and turned around to face all of us below, the shouting stopped as people tried to figure out why he was there.

"Second," he said, "my own name is on top of the list. I will not ask anyone to do anything I cannot do myself."

These words were greeted with shock. Director Steven had volunteered. How could anyone else refuse if his or her name was drawn?

Mom stepped forward.

"No!" I cried. "Don't go!"

She turned around. Tears ran down her face, but she smiled. "Tyce, more than anything I want you to choose to believe in God—to realize that life beyond the body is more important than anything else, and that, with God waiting in heaven for you, you don't have to fear death. I've told you before that Jesus, who died for you, loves you intensely. I love you too."

Mom left me and slowly moved to the ladder that led up to the platform buggy deck.

She began to climb. Away from me. And toward her own death.

To think of Mom giving up her life to save me and the others of the dome was to understand a love that felt like a sword piercing my heart. To think of her gone made me so empty that I almost couldn't breathe.

In that moment, I understood a bit of what she'd been trying to tell me all along. There was something inside me that no scientific instrument could measure or explain. Had I really been created by a God who cared—for *me?*

Without realizing that my arms had moved, I felt the rims of my wheels in the palms of my hands.

Without saying a word, I pushed forward in my wheelchair and forward to the platform buggy. If Mom trusted in God, then I too would trust that my soul had a place to go.

She heard the sounds of my wheels squeaking.

She turned. Shock filled her face.

"No!"

"Yes," I said. "I don't care if I'm needed for the robot experiments. If you go, I go."

We were whispering because it was deathly still. With all two hundred people watching us, not a single voice spoke.

Mom pivoted and looked upward at Director Steven on the platform buggy deck.

"Make him stay behind," she begged. "Have the guards stun him so he cannot follow. I am trading my life for his."

More heartbeats of silence.

Director Steven checked the sheet of paper in his hand.

"I cannot let him stay behind," he said. "When I drew names, I did not set anyone apart. Because of that, his name is on this list too."

CHAPTER 20

We slowly traveled across the Martian landscape, ten of us in one platform buggy and ten in the other, following closely behind. Except for me and Director Steven, two security guards, and the two tekkies who first volunteered to leave the dome, the rest were scientists.

After the entire list had been read, Rawling had tried to volunteer. Rawling had said there were too many important scientists, too many of the best brains in the solar system about to die. Rawling had said it wasn't right, and he should at least be allowed to take the place of one of those scientists. Director Steven had said that the decisions had been made and the names drawn in all fairness. We were to proceed accordingly.

One of the security guards whose name had been drawn tried to make a run for it, but was stun-blasted by two others and hauled up into the platform buggy.

Just like me. Only I wasn't hauled up because I had been trying to get away. Without the use of my legs, I couldn't climb. So a big security guard had thrown me over his shoulder like a sack and carried me up the ladder. Another security guard had brought up my wheelchair. Not that it made a difference. There wasn't much room to move around in the platform buggy observation deck. The doors weren't locked, but with no space suits and an atmosphere of carbon dioxide waiting outside, there was no place to go.

All of that had taken place a half-hour earlier.

Now we were at least twenty miles clear of the dome. The inside of our platform buggy was very quiet, except for the humming of the electric motor that powered the monstrous wheels beneath us.

Mom sat, hugging her knees, at one end of the dome. A security guard was at the steering wheel. The other seven scientists were scattered in different groups, whispering among themselves. Director Steven was driving the other platform buggy, with the nine other people for passengers.

As for me, I was beside Mom, in my wheelchair by the clear glass window at the edge of the platform buggy dome. I let my hands mindlessly juggle the red balls as I stared out at the landscape.

The sun began to drop behind the distant mountains. Our dome was on a valley plain. Towering above the nearby hills, those mountains stood fifty thousand feet high, black and jagged and awesome against the sun.

I've been told that sunsets on Earth can be incredible. A mixture of reds, oranges, and pinks all streak across the sky.

Not so on Mars.

Since there's so little atmosphere, there are few particles of dust or smoke to work as prisms to change the sun's light into different colors as the sun nears the horizon. Here on Mars, the sun always looks like a blue ball of fire.

What's incredible, however, are the pinks and reds and roses of the land itself. With its red soil and the salmon color of the sky, the beauty of the desolate landscape is haunting and sad.

Of course, part of the reason I felt that way as I looked through the clear bubble of the platform buggy was a result of seeing where all of us were headed. Director Steven said he didn't want the others back at the dome to be reminded of what would happen to us. So we'd have to travel out of sight of the dome and then park, waiting for our oxygen to run out.

CHAPTER 21

The strangest thing happened the next morning.

I woke up. Alive.

Mom had prayed for us the night before, because we both expected that, during the night, the oxygen in the platform buggy would run out. Usually only two or three people went out in it at a time, so it did not carry enough oxygen for the ten of us for a long period. We expected to go to sleep and never wake up.

As I blinked and rubbed my eyes, I saw surprise on the other faces as well.

We didn't have a chance to wonder about it for long.

"Good morning, everyone." Director Steven's voice came over the communication speaker, talking to us from the other platform buggy. "Please make sure you all have breakfast. I want all of you to remain as healthy as possible."

I gave Mom a strange look. She gave me a strange look.

Wearing the jumpsuit I'd fallen asleep in, I rolled over on the floor and pulled myself into my wheelchair.

"To those of you who are surprised to be breathing this morning," his cheerful voice continued, "please let me apologize for yesterday's drama. Let me assure you that neither platform buggy will run short of oxygen until the supply ship arrives from Earth."

I pushed over to the window, fighting to move the wheels as I'd been doing over the last few weeks.

I stared across the space between the platform buggies. I could see into the other platform buggy where Director Steven was facing the microphone.

"Let me explain," Director Steven said calmly. "The oxygen level in the dome is far lower than anyone knew. Had I been truthful about it, there would have been panic and civil war as people fought for the remaining oxygen tanks. After I did all the calculations, I discovered there was only enough oxygen for twenty people to survive."

He cleared his throat. "That left a simple problem. How could I get those twenty out of the dome without the other 180 fighting to go? You have probably guessed by now how I came to a simple solution. I made it appear as if these twenty were the ones who would die. That way, no one would stop them from leaving. And you, of course, are the twenty. Mercifully, the others left in the dome will not face the fear that comes with knowing the oxygen will run short. They will just become sleepy and die peacefully."

What? I thought wildly.

"The few of you who volunteered to give up your lives are here because you deserve to live. The rest of you are among the greatest scientific minds in the solar system. I made a decision that you must be spared to continue the Mars Project."

What?

Director Steven glanced across the short space between the platform buggies. He caught me staring at him in surprise.

"You, too, Tyce," Director Steven said. Surprisingly, he

smiled at me. "We cannot afford to lose you. Not after you proved yesterday that the experimental robots can be controlled by human brains."

A hundred and eighty people had been condemned to die, just to save the few of us?

"Rest assured, people," Director Steven finished in his smooth voice, "we do have enough oxygen. The tanks that were taken a few nights ago were hidden on these platform buggies. The two men who assisted in that task are the two security guards among us. In fact, one even pretended to resist entering the platform buggy, just to make it look more realistic that all of us were headed for death. Of course, no one else in the dome knows any of this. But those of us in the platform buggies will survive. None of you should feel guilt, as this was my decision and you had no choice in the matter."

The speakers in our platform buggy clicked off as Director Steven hung up his microphone.

Back at the dome, time and air were running out for everyone. Including Rawling McTigre, the one man I trusted above everybody else.

CHAPTER 22

On the other side of our platform buggy, the security guard was handing out nutri-tubes for breakfast.

I struggled to push my wheelchair over there. It had been getting more and more difficult to move. I wondered if Director Steven had lied to us about the oxygen, just so we'd die peacefully and without fear.

When I reached the security guard, he gave me my choice of scrambled eggs and bacon, or scrambled eggs and sausage.

"Like there's a difference," I said.

He grinned. "Good point."

He was square-shouldered, with a brush cut and a squashed nose, as if it had once been broken.

"Scissors?" he asked.

"No, thank you," I said. As usual, I just ripped open the top of the tube.

"Hey, muscles," he teased, laughing, "promise you won't get mad at me."

"Ha, ha," I said. I pushed away and found a spot near the edge of the observation deck. If breakfast had to taste bad, at least I could eat it where I had a nice view.

I'd slept for nearly ten hours and the sun was already above the horizon, casting long shadows from the jagged rocks that littered the Martian sand.

Then it hit me. If the reason I struggled to push my wheelchair was because of lack of oxygen, how come I could still rip open a nutri-tube?

I thought back over the last few days. Not once had I been forced to use scissors on the nutri-tubes.

So maybe it wasn't my hands and arms getting weak.

But why then was it still difficult to push my wheelchair?

I thought about that as I slowly chewed and swallowed the gooey yellow paste that was called scrambled eggs and bacon.

Mom moved beside me and sat on the floor to eat her breakfast.

"I'm still in shock," she said. "Director Steven had this planned out for a long time. Early enough to steal the oxygen tanks and pretend he knew nothing about it."

"Yeah," I said, my mind on my wheelchair.

"I'm curious what you think," Mom said thoughtfully. "Is what he did right? I mean, Director Steven—"

"Can you help me out of my wheelchair?" I asked, interrupting her.

"Sure, but—"

"Now?" I asked.

I gave her what was left of my nutri-tube.

Mom set it aside and lifted me out of the chair by grabbing under my armpits. She set me on the floor. I leaned my back against the glass of the platform buggy wall.

"Thanks," I said.

"Tyce?" she asked. "What is it?"

I spun the back of the wheelchair toward me. There was

a small tool kit underneath the seat that made it possible to take the wheelchair apart and put it back together.

"Give me one minute," I said, reaching for the tool kit. "I'll tell you if I'm right about something."

I tilted the wheelchair on its side. I undid the bolt that attached the wheel to the axle and took the wheel off.

The other scientists were in their own discussions and didn't pay much attention. After all, they were the greatest minds in the solar system. To them I was just a kid. A crippled kid.

With the wheel in my lap, I used a screwdriver to dig out the bearings that let the wheel turn on the axle.

I tried to spin the bearings.

They hardly moved.

That, at least, explained why it had been so hard to move my wheelchair.

And that also explained why the solar panels would not work properly. Suddenly I knew, without a shadow of a doubt, what the problem was!

I put the wheelchair together as quickly as I could, had Mom help me back into my wheelchair, and then approached the security guard.

CHAPTER 23

"Director Steven," I pleaded, "you have to let them know."

I was at the console of our platform buggy, speaking into my headset. Director Steven sat at the console of his platform buggy, also wearing a headset. I'd just finished telling Director Steven about what had happened to my wheelchair and the ball bearings. They'd been ground down, probably by the microscopic silicon of Martian sand, making them hard to move. What if the wheels on the solar panels had the same problem?

He looked across at me. The platform buggies were parked side by side in the shade of a hill.

"No," he said, meeting my eyes directly.

"No?"

"They already believe we're dead. It'll cause panic if they find out we're still alive."

"But this can save them!" I said.

"You aren't sure of that."

"No, but—"

I was talking in a low voice. The security guard who had set me up at the console was standing at the opposite wall because I'd asked him if I could have a private conversation with Director Steven.

"But nothing," Director Steven said. He ran his hands through his hair. "Already their oxygen levels are dangerously low. Even if they fixed the panels now, the generators wouldn't produce enough oxygen to save them."

"We could drive back," I pleaded. "We could share our oxygen with them as they wait for the generators to make more oxygen."

"I will not gamble these twenty lives on another wild guess of yours," Director Steven said. "If you're wrong and we go back and share our oxygen, we too will die. It's that simple."

"But—"

"But nothing. We sit here and wait. There will be no communication with the dome. Am I clear?"

"But—"

"Am I clear?"

I pulled off my headset and smiled.

The security guard came back to the console and took the headset from me.

"Well?" he asked. "Did you get what you wanted?"

"Sure did," I said. I reached for the switch that would link our platform buggy radio with the main radio back at the dome. I flipped it on as if there was no question about it.

The security guard frowned.

"I didn't think there was supposed to be any communication with home base," he said.

"I just talked to Director Steven about it," I said. Which was true.

I leaned forward and spoke clearly into the radio microphone.

"Platform buggy one to home base. Tell Rawling McTigre

to talk to Tyce. Platform buggy one to home base. Tell Rawling McTigre to talk to Tyce. Platform buggy one to home base. Tell Rawling—"

"Grab that kid!" It was Director Steven shouting into the speaker of his platform buggy, his voice echoing in ours. "Shut him up! Now!"

The security guard pulled me away so quickly that I almost fell out of my wheelchair.

Director Steven stood at the glass wall of his platform buggy, glaring at me. All other eyes in both platform buggies stared at me.

"Sit him in a corner and make sure he doesn't move." Director Steven's voice was thick with rage. "If he tries anything else, put him outside. Without a space suit."

CHAPTER 24

It took five minutes for the scientists in our platform buggy to forget about me and Director Steven's threat.

Mom drew up a chair beside my wheelchair.

"What was all that about?" she asked softly.

"I wish I had time to explain," I said. "But I need to go to sleep as fast as possible."

"Tyce?"

"Can you trust me on this, Mom? I need to sit here with my eyes closed. Turn my wheelchair around so no one can see my face. Make sure nobody comes by and disturbs me. That's all I ask."

"For how long?"

"Until I wake up," I said. "Please?"

She sighed. "This is so strange."

"So is letting all those people die."

Without a word, she turned me away from the other people in the buggy. My view was of the back side of the hill. Rock and sand in all colors of brown and red and black.

I closed my eyes and waited in the wired jumpsuit I was still wearing from when I left the dome. I hoped and prayed that someone at the dome had heard my short message. I hoped and prayed that Rawling would understand what I meant. I hoped and prayed that very soon, in the darkness of my mind, I would fall off the edge of a high, invisible cliff into a deep, invisible hole.

"Tyce?"

"Took you long enough," I said to Rawling.

I tilted my video head and peered into his face. His skin was gray, and he was sweating badly. I clicked around the room—slowly, to keep from getting dizzy—with my other three video lenses to see if anyone else was with us.

"Someone heard your broadcast and called me in my mini-dome," he said. "I tried to radio the platform buggy, but I didn't get an answer. If you wanted me to turn on the robot, why not say so instead of making me figure it out?"

"Because," I answered. I spun my robot wheels back and forth, warming up. "Then Director Steven would have known how I intended to talk to you. And he would have stopped me."

Rawling wiped his face. His jumpsuit was blotched with sweat. "You guys are supposed to be dead."

"Long story," I said. I looked around the lab and found the tools I needed. I handed them to Rawling. "I will tell you after. But we need to get to the solar panels."

"Sure," he said, "but I don't feel so good. Maybe we can get someone else to help you."

I reached across and pinched his shin bone with my titanium fingers.

"Ouch!" he said, shocked.

"You have got to stay awake. The lack of oxygen is starting to get to you."

"Lack of oxygen? But—"

"You don't have much time. Follow me."

I wheeled forward. I got to the door of the lab. I tried twisting the knob with my fingers. I twisted too hard. It fell off in my hand.

"Oops," I said. "I do not know my own strength."

I wheeled back and picked up a chair with both hands. I held it in front of me.

I crashed into the door with it. The door popped open.

Checking behind me with my rear lens, I made sure Rawling was following me. He staggered slightly as he tried to keep up.

"It is the wheels of the solar panels," I explained quickly. "The panels work fine. But if the railing wheels are stuck even slightly, the panels cannot track the sun's movement as they slide along the roof of the dome. They do not have the right angle to catch enough sunlight to produce power."

I noticed no one was walking around the dome.

"Where is everybody?" I asked.

"I think sleeping," he said. "Which is what I want to do."

Continuing forward, I reached back with one arm. I grabbed Rawling's hand.

"Ouch," he said again.

I didn't let go.

"You are coming with me."

I led him up the ramp to the second-floor walkway, then along the walkway. Soon we were at the ladders that reached up to the solar panels.

"You will have to climb," I said. "I cannot. All you need to do is disconnect two or three wheels from the solar panel railing. Bring them back down."

He nodded, slowly.

As I waited below, I scanned the dome. No movement anywhere. Were people already dying?

I switched to infrared and scanned the nearest mini-dome.

The mini-dome itself was a light red, showing that it held slightly more heat than the cool air of the dome. Inside, a deep glowing red in the form of a body showed me where someone rested on the bed. I watched carefully and saw a slight rising and falling of the form. The person was still breathing.

Switching off infrared, I went to the visual light spectrum, seeing colors as normally viewed by human eyes. I swiveled my video lens upward at Rawling. He was nearly finished taking off a couple of wheels.

I hoped I was right in my guess.

If I was wrong, I'd be in my robot body, helpless to prevent all these people from dying over the next few hours.

CHAPTER 25

I blinked open my eyes in the platform buggy.

There was noise and excitement behind me.

I spun in my wheelchair.

Everyone was gathered at the far window, staring down from the platform buggy at the desert floor.

I smiled. I knew what had their attention.

I wheeled up beside them.

"It's a robot," I said loudly.

My words quieted them down.

One of the scientists frowned at me. "Of course it's a robot," he said. "We aren't stupid. We want to know what it's doing here. Five minutes ago, I saw it coming here at a speed I estimated to be forty miles an hour. Then suddenly it stopped in front of our platform buggies. And what's that in its hands?"

"Solar panel wheels," I said. "Damaged solar panel wheels. I'm not totally sure it's from microscopic particles of Martian sand, but that's my best guess. I think over the years, the sand has seeped into the dome. I do know that my own wheelchair can hardly move because the ball bearings have been ground down, and the only reason I can come up with is sand."

I had everyone's attention.

"The solar panels follow the sun," I said. "If the wheels on the solar panel railings have the tiniest bit of drag, the solar panels will always be a few degrees behind the best angle to catch maximum sun. I think that's what's been happening. Slowly, the generators have been dying. Not because anything is wrong with the panels. But because something's wrong with the wheels."

A voice interrupted me.

"What's the discussion in there?" Director Steven asked from the other platform buggy.

"Mom, could you turn the speaker down and let me finish? Then all of you can decide what to do. . . ."

"I'll turn it down," another scientist volunteered. "This is all so crazy, there must be some truth in it."

"Thank you," I said. It hurt my head to look up at everybody from my wheelchair. "That robot brought back a few of the wheels from the dome to prove that's the problem. We need to return to the dome. We can replace the wheels and begin generating electricity within hours. The people in there don't have to die."

From the corner of my eye, I saw Director Steven waving wildly, trying to get our attention. I ignored him and explained more.

"The oxygen levels in the dome are so low that everyone has passed out. They need oxygen from the platform buggy reserves to survive until the generators kick in again. It'll take about an hour to return. That's just enough time to save them."

"And if you're wrong," another scientist said, "we'll have given them the oxygen that would keep us alive."

"That's why I brought back the solar panel wheels," I said. "To prove it to you."

A third scientist snorted through his thick white beard. "You brought them back? That's a robot out there. You've been here in your wheelchair, asleep. Now I understand why Director Steven thinks you're dangerous. You've lost your mind."

I'd forgotten. The experiments with the robot were so recent that only Mom, Rawling, and the director knew about them.

I grinned at all the people staring at me.

"I think," I said, "I have a way to prove to you that I'm in control of the robot."

CHAPTER 26

It had become a beautiful sensation, falling off the edge of a high, invisible cliff into a deep, invisible hole.

When the falling ended, I focused my video lens upward at the platform buggy observation deck. I saw nine people crowded at the glass wall, peering down on me. Behind them, I knew, my motionless body sat in my wheelchair.

The heat of the Martian sun seemed to glow in my titanium bones. It was midday, and the temperature registered 65 degrees Fahrenheit. In my entire life, I'd never been outside. It felt as marvelous now as it had when I'd first left the dome to scoot across the plains.

And wind. I'd never heard the sound of wind. Only read about it. It whistled across the stark rocks embedded in the Martian sand. Tiny bits of sand rattled off my wheels and arms as I sped across the landscape. It was such a glorious feeling of being alive.

I wanted to sit where I was and enjoy all of this—the things that humans on Earth can have anytime, just by stepping outside. But I'd made a promise to the scientists in the platform buggy. And they, in return, had made a promise to me.

If I could convince them I was the brains of this robot, they'd follow me back to the dome and share their oxygen with the others.

First I raised one titanium hand and waved.

They hadn't expected this. I could see on their faces that a few were startled. Others waved back, big smiles on their faces.

I waved at Director Steven in the other dome.

He crossed his arms and frowned at me.

I stopped waving. My left hand held two solar panel wheels, small like the wheels of roller blades on Earth. I dropped my right hand, which held one wheel, down to the ground. Holding the wheel tight between two fingers, I dragged my other titanium finger as I began to move the robot back and forth.

When I was finished, I surveyed my handwriting in the Martian sand. TAKE US HOME, it said in big letters.

I looked up again and saw that many were pointing down. They could see it clearly, and they understood.

But that wasn't all I'd promised as proof.

I turned the robot to face all of them as they watched me from the observatory decks of both platform buggies.

In my mind, I took a deep breath. Breathing was one of the few things I did better in my own crippled body than I did in the robot body. Still, just thinking of breathing helped me concentrate. I wanted to do this right. I wanted to be able to lead them to the dome across the packed sand of the desert that let this robot run like it was a leopard.

All eyes were on me as I began to deliver on my promise to them.

I switched the small solar panel wheel from my right hand into my left hand, so that my left hand held all three wheels.

Then I tossed one of the small solar panel wheels in the air with my left hand. I caught it with my right, but as I was catching that wheel, I tossed the second wheel from my left hand into the air. A split second later, I tossed the third wheel.

And just like that, I was juggling.

EPILOGUE

We did it. We made it back to the dome just in time.

All of us worked together to fix the solar panels and give oxygen to the people who were on the verge of slipping away.

I was right. Microscopic sand particles were the problem. It had taken years and years, but eventually the buildup of sand and the wearing down of the ball bearings had made the solar panel wheels drag just slightly—enough to throw off the panel angles. So now that the ball bearings have been fixed, there's no longer a danger of anyone dying from lack of oxygen.

After the immediate threat of death was gone, the people turned their attention elsewhere . . . to Director Steven.

Everybody under the dome is angry at him. And who can blame them? In the same way that he used my body as an experiment by forcing my mom to let a surgeon put a rod in my spine, Director Steven used all of the tekkies and workers as pieces of a puzzle, shifting them around to suit what he thought the Project needed. Whether he was right or wrong, the dome scientists disagree.

But the fact is, no one trusts him now. Soon the next supply ship will arrive. When it leaves to go back to Earth, he'll be shipped back with it. Rawling has been voted in as the new Mars Project director.

I do feel sorry for ex-Director Steven. He faced a difficult decision in trying to choose who should live and who should die. But I think that was just it. He made the decision without talking to anyone, as if he were trying to be God.

After facing death, learning how I really became crippled, and seeing my mom's willingness to sacrifice her life for me, I'm a lot more open about that subject too.

The subject of God.

Mom has always said faith is a sure hope in things unseen.

I've decided that just because I can't find a way to measure the existence of God, it doesn't mean he isn't there.

And it's the same thing with the soul.

Actually, all of this has helped me stop feeling sorry for myself in my wheelchair. I've realized something.

All of us, even the best athletes, are imprisoned by our bodies. Against our will, our bodies will someday grow old or sick. And, sadly, our bodies will die.

When I think of it that way, I'm in the same prison you are. Sure, in an uncrippled body, your prison cell might be bigger and brighter, but not by much. You can run at eight miles an hour, and I can only roll along in my wheelchair at three miles an hour, and in my robot body I can go three times as fast as you. But all of those speeds are so tiny compared to the vastness of the universe that it doesn't matter at all who's faster.

But what I've begun to understand is that, although we're stuck in our bodies, we can have freedom of the soul. The kind of freedom my mom has found, through her faith in Jesus Christ. I don't know how she got it, but maybe someday I'll find out for myself.

. . . Anyway, I've got to shut down this computer and go. Rawling—I mean, Director Rawling—is yelling to me about someone seeing aliens outside of the dome.

Ha. Aliens. Not very likely.

But Rawling is insisting I get into the robot body and do a quick search.

Although I'm excited about getting outside on the surface of Mars again, I'm not expecting to find anything.

Everybody knows there aren't any aliens on Mars.

Right?

WHAT DOES SCIENCE TELL US ABOUT GOD?

Does God really exist?

Tyce Sanders wondered, and you might, too. As Tyce points out in this book, if you're looking for measured proof that God exists, science has been unable to find it.

Or has it?

For centuries, science and faith have seemed to be poles apart. Much of this happened because of how the church in Rome treated a scientist named Galileo in the early 1700s. Galileo publicly supported a new theory that the Earth revolved around the sun. But the church insisted the Bible said otherwise. As a result, the pope punished Galileo—he even threatened to have Galileo killed unless he began to teach again that the sun revolved around the Earth. From that point on, many "religious" people saw scientists as people who wanted to attack religion; and scientists became anti-religion.

What the people didn't know was that someday Galileo, who deeply believed in God, would be known as one of the greatest scientists of all time. He foresaw that a new invention, the telescope, would prove the church wrong—as it did. He wanted to save them from the embarrassment of supporting the wrong theory. But they wouldn't listen.

Because of this divide, it seems that we today have two choices: accept God on the merit of faith, choosing to believe what the Bible says (that God does exist and loves us individually) or believe what science claims to prove (that there is no God).

However, over the last fifty years, science has admitted that every discovery leads to more questions than answers. A century ago, many scientists believed they were on the verge of knowing all the answers regarding how we arrived on this planet called Earth. Now scientists say that the more they discover, the more they discover they don't know.

For example, if the force of gravity were slightly more, the universe would collapse on itself, like a balloon with the air sucked out of it. If the force of gravity were slightly less, it would have drifted apart as gases, instead of forming solids. If the force that held protons and electrons together were the slightest bit weaker, hydrogen would not exist, and therefore water would not exist, and therefore life would not exist. At all levels, it seems that coincidence after coincidence after coincidence has made human life possible in a lonely, cold universe.[1]

Yet are they coincidences? Scientists have tried different computer models to simulate the creation of a universe that could sustain life. They can only find one model that works: ours, with the incredible adjustments of creation that truly are difficult to believe as mere concidence. As a result, many scientists are led to faith in God because of what they see in the universe—an amazingly complex interworking of humans, plants, animals, stars, etc. It can only be the product of careful design by a loving creator.

Many scientists now believe that the fifteen-billion-year

construction of the universe has had one goal: producing human life. Now that should make you feel special! Science is proving that the odds of human life being produced by chance are like winning the same ten-million-dollar lottery every week for the next year. (That's a big win!) So the next time you hear people complain that they didn't win the lottery, tell them they already did.

It's true that belief in God truly takes a leap of faith, and, as Tyce told his mother, no one can force you to believe. Yet every year we see further proof that science—and reason—no longer stand in the way of a belief in God as the creator of this universe.

What an awesome thought—that a loving God created and sustains the universe, and cares for you personally!

[1]For a full list of these "coincidences," read the book *Universes*, by John Leslie (London: Routledge, 1989). For further reading, check out *God, The Evidence*, by Patrick Glynn (Prima Publishing, 1997).

ABOUT THE AUTHOR

Sigmund Brouwer and his wife, recording artist Cindy Morgan, split living between Red Deer, Alberta, Canada, and Nashville, Tennessee. He has written several series of juvenile fiction and eight novels. Sigmund loves sports and plays golf and hockey. He also enjoys visiting schools to talk about books. He welcomes visitors to his Web site at www.coolreading.com, where he and a bunch of other authors like to hang out in cyberspace.

MARS
DIARIES
are you ready?

Set in an experimental community on Mars, the Mars Diaries feature 14-year-old Tyce Sanders. Life on the red planet is not always easy, but it is definitely exciting. As Tyce explores his strange surroundings, he also finds that the mysteries of the planet point to his greatest discovery—a new relationship with God.

MISSION 1: OXYGEN LEVEL ZERO
Can Tyce stop the oxygen leak in time?

MISSION 2: ALIEN PURSUIT
What attacked the tekkie in the lab?

MISSION 3: TIME BOMB
What mystery is uncovered by the quake?

MISSION 4: HAMMERHEAD
Will the comet crash on Earth, destroying all life?

MISSION 5: SOLE SURVIVOR
Will a hostile takeover destroy the Mars Project?

MISSION 6: MOON RACER
Who's really controlling the spaceship?

MISSION 7: COUNTDOWN
Will there be enough time to save the others?

MISSION 8: ROBOT WAR
Will the rebels succeed with their plan?

MISSIONS 9 & 10 COMING SOON